This book belongs to:

_____

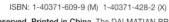

06 07 08 LPU 10 9 8 7 6 5 4 3 2 — 14282 Hanna-Barbera - Classic Cartoon Collection

Hanna-Barbera™

CLASSIC CARTOON COLLECTION

SCOOBY-DOO!

THE HAUNTED CARNIVAL

Story by Ronald Kidd

Drawings by Vaccaro Associates, Inc. and Eric Binder

One summer day Scooby-Doo, Shaggy, Fred, Daphne, Velma, and Scrappy-Doo decided to take a break from detective work and go to a carnival.

"Like, let's investigate what kind of food they have," Shaggy suggested.

Shaggy, Scooby, and Scrappy followed their noses to the hotdog stand as the others went to find fun games to play.

With hotdogs in hand, Shaggy, Scooby, and Scrappy boarded the roller coaster.

As they got to the top of the tracks Scrappy-Doo noticed that the old ride attendant had disappeared. There was no one to slow down the cars as they headed toward a big curve! Quickly, Scrappy jumped from the car, climbed down the ride, and pushed the brake lever to "Stop."

"That was, like, too close for comfort," said Shaggy when he and Scooby were safely on the ground.

Meanwhile, Velma, Fred, and Daphne were trying their luck at a dart game.

On her very first try, Velma popped a balloon. But the ballon was filled with paint that splattered everywhere!

"Hey! What kind of prank is this?" Daphne demanded. She looked for the man who had been running the game, but he was gone.

The whole gang met up and traded stories. Since something strange was definitely going on, they decided to stay together. They were watching Mr. and Mrs. Gullet perform their sword-swallowing act until it was interrupted by a large cloud of smoke.

POOF! A masked figure appeared. "I am the Phantom of the Carnival!" he yelled. "I warn you—disaster will strike! Run before it's too late!" Then he vanished in another cloud of smoke. The crowd panicked and ran for the gates.

Soon the carnival grounds were quiet and it was getting dark. But Scooby and the gang didn't leave. They knew that they had a mystery to solve.

Mr. and Mrs. Gullet explained that they had recently become owners of the carnival. "This Phantom is scaring away our customers!" Mr. Gullet complained.

Just then, a noise came from the House of Mirrors.
"Let's go!" shouted fearless Scrappy-Doo as he rushed inside.
Scrappy lunged at an image of the Phantom and slammed nose-first into a mirror.
"Ha! Ha! You'll never catch me!" chuckled the Phantom as he ran down a hallway.

Instead of joining in the chase, Scooby crouched down and covered his head to hide. But when the Phantom ran back down the hall he tripped over Scooby and fell to the floor. Mr. Gullet reached down and pulled off the Phantom's mask.

"Jinkies! That's the man from the dart game!" Velma exclaimed.

"It's Scotty, one of our workers!" said Mrs. Gullet.

"Why have you done this, Scotty?" asked Mr. Gullet.

"I wanted to buy the carnival," said Scotty. "I thought if I scared everyone away you might sell it to me. And it would have worked if it weren't for you kids and your mangy dogs!"

"Like, Scooby to the rescue!" Shaggy said as he gave Scooby-Doo a hug.

"Rappy, roo!" said Scooby-Doo happily as he smiled at his cousin.

The end!

Now Museum, Now You Don't!

Story by Charles Carney

Drawings by Spike Brandt, Tony Cervone, and Ryan Dunlavey

The shiny brass sign that hung above Tom's bed said "348 Days Without a Mouse."

Every morning he polished it, and every night, right before he went to bed, Tom would change the number. For this was the world's most mouse-free museum, and so it would stay. This watchcat took pride in his work.

Jerry was returning from almost a year's journey around the world. He had ridden on airplanes across the oceans, traveled by train through the mountains, and been driven around in taxis in all the big cities. He was the best-traveled mouse in the world. Why, just look at his suitcase stickers!

Now he was back to his home in the museum. "Well," he thought, "they must have missed me terribly to install such a splendid plaque as this one." Jerry felt very welcomed and began to polish the brass plaque. "I wonder what this month's exhibit is?" he asked himself.

Not Jerry! He ran and s—l—i—i—i—d down the waxed corridor. Tom took-off after him, but couldn't get any traction on the slick floor! He was going nowhere fast, so he decided to creep in kitty-cat fashion. He guessed Jerry was hiding in the Mummy Room, so he crept in oh—so—s—l—o—w—l—y.

"Aaaagh!" A hideous face appeared from nowhere. The cat leaped as high as he could and grabbed the ceiling fan. Jerry switched it on. Tom swung wildly, his legs knocking over Mummy cases one... two... three... four... five... eight... twelve... twenty! They clattered and clanked and fell, fell, fell.

Tom's eyes danced with excitement at the thought of 349 days without a mouse. He sprang into the next room—but no Jerry. All he found was a tiny, scribbled-in-red sign reading "PULL THIS LEVER." Tom's curiosity got the better of him. He's a cat. He knew he shouldn't do it. Everything in him said not to do it. But he pulled the lever anyway.

Tom heard a rumble and looked up to see shelf upon shelf, floor to ceiling—an exhibit called "A Thousand Years of Cannonballs"— suddenly thundering down toward him. He'd pulled the RELEASE lever! Tom was fast, but rolling cannonballs are faster! Jerry stood by counting the number of clangs!

The cannonballs swept through an exhibit of statues, running into everything. Tom rode them like a clumsy circus acrobat. Faster, he headed for the window, grabbing left and right for something to slow him down. What could possibly keep him from rolling right out the window?

A stairway, that's what! Tom rode the cannonball waterfall over the edge. CRASH! BOOM! BASH! When the stars around his head cleared, he was sitting in a darkened room. He couldn't see a thing. Then he heard it. GRRRRRRRR! Something growled like a very big dog. Uh-oh.

ROOOOOAR!! He couldn't believe his ears. Tom turned on the lights. Where were they? Thunder clapped and the lights blinked. He heard a wolf go OOOWWWOOOOO! Then RAT—A—TAT—TAT—TAT! went a machine gun! Whistling bombs went BOOOOOM! Then...

...ringing telephones? The lights came on and there stood Jerry, laughing. They were in a SOUND EFFECTS exhibit. Tom was *steamed*. He felt his temperature rise like mercury in a thermometer.

Then his ears buzzed, which only added to his bad mood.

He shook his head, but the buzz only got louder. Then ZOOM! Something went by fast. Then SWOOP! something else! WHIZZZZIP! He was being dive-bombed by a fleet of toy airplanes! And Jerry was leading the attack, bombing Tom with a water balloon.

Tom grabbed the "Y" from the "POWER TOYS" sign and put a rubber band across the top of it. He took a lightbulb and launched it with his homemade slingshot. Pop! A direct hit! One of the toy planes spun out of control and bounced into the wall.

KER-RACK! POW! Down it went!

He fired off two more. But Jerry was a clever little pilot. After all the other planes had fallen, Jerry was still in the air, dipping and dodging and bombarding Tom with marbles.

Yeowch! Ow! Eeek!
Tom grabbed a helmet from the VIRTUAL WORLD exhibit, put it on and fastened it tight. Now he was protected.

He turned to face Jerry, but without warning, everything took on an eery glow.

Tom was now in a Virtual World — and Jerry had the remote control!

Jerry programmed Tom into "Virtual Auto-Racing."
Zoom! Tom ran around in little circles. Jerry pressed "Virtual Rodeo" and Tom bucked and bounced around the room.

Then Jerry tried "Virtual Outer Space." Tom started moving more slowly. His hands went up in the air.

He stood on his tiptoes. Then he began to float! Jerry walked over and opened the window, and Tom, still in the helmet, floated outside, higher and higher toward the full moon as Jerry waved bye-bye!

The end!

THE FLINTSTONES™

NO BIZ LIKE SHOW BIZ

Story by Dandi Mackall & Scott Awley
Illustrated by Scott Jeralds and Darryl Goudreau

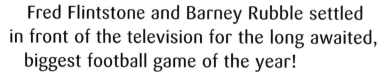

Fred Flintstone and Barney Rubble settled in front of the television for the long awaited, biggest football game of the year!

"Phone's off! Shades are pulled," said Barney.

"Great! We're all set! Yabba-Dabba-Doo," exclaimed Fred.

"This game is gonna be great!"

CHOMP, CHOMP, CHOMP! Dino chomped on his favorite bone. "Cut that out, Dino! I want absolute quiet around here for the next hour! Go play outside!" Fred screamed. Poor Dino whimpered, and dragged his bone into the front yard.

BAM! BAM! PLUNK! Pebbles and Bamm-Bamm were playing with their toy musical instruments. "Wilma!" yelled Fred. "Will you *please* take Pebbles and Bamm-Bamm out of here?"

"The kids are making an awful racket," exclaimed Barney. Betty and Wilma rushed to the rescue. "All this fuss over football sure makes you wonder who the kids are around here," said Betty.

"Let's humor them before they have a fit," said Wilma.

Fred finally settled in and turned on the TV. THUMP! THUMP! YEAH! Teenage rock music was on every channel! The final straw came when they heard the TV announcer say, *"Bedrock's Game of the Year is postponed to bring you this special program."*

"Postponed!" Fred and Barney yelled together. "Oh, no!" The announcer continued: *"Today we are interviewing the world-famous teenage rock star manager, Mr. Rock Kidd!"*

"They can't do this to us! We're missing the game! Who's running this country?" Fred protested. "Teenagers or us?"

"Looks like they are, Fred," Barney answered.

"Barney's right," Fred muttered. "Teenagers are taking over! I'm glad we've got normal kids with no talent!"

Barney went home to mow the lawn, and Fred dozed off for an afternoon nap.

No sooner had Fred started to snore, when he awoke to loud rock music! Fred jerked straight up from the couch at what sounded like teenagers singing! He stormed outside. "Teenagers rehearsing in my backyard! Some nerve!"

Fred stormed outside to put a stop to the racket. But instead of teenagers, Fred found Pebbles and Bamm-Bamm making beautiful music! "Yikes! Those aren't teenagers, that's Pebbles and Bamm-Bamm!" Fred shouted. "Barney! Barney! Come quick!"

Barney rushed over. "I can't believe it, Fred! Pebbles and Bamm-Bamm are singing! And they can't even talk yet!"

"Yabba-Dabba-Doo!" said Fred. "You know what this means, pal? We're going to be millionaires!"

Fred and Barney called Wilma and Betty to tell them the good news. But when the girls showed up, they watched as Pebbles said her usual "Da Da!" Bamm-Bamm thrashed at the drum with only a "Bamm-Bamm!"

"Well, Fred?" Wilma asked. "'You expect 'Da Da' to make the top ten?" she giggled.

"If you'll excuse us, boys," said Betty, "Wilma and I are busy." The girls giggled and walked away.

"Do you think we imagined the whole thing, Fred?" asked Barney.

"How can you hear what I imagined?" replied Fred.

Just then the doorbell rang. There stood the rock star manager, Rock Kidd!

"May I use your telephone?" asked Rock. "Having a bit of car trouble!"

All of a sudden, the kids' music started again! "Where is that sound coming from?" Rock asked. "Those kids are fab! Who is that?"

Fred, Barney, Wilma, Betty and Rock ran to the backyard. "That's my little girl on guitar!" exclaimed a proud Fred. "And that's my boy on drums!" said Barney.

"The boys were telling the truth, Betty!" said Wilma.

"Pebbles and Bamm-Bamm are actually singing!"

"Leave it to me, Mr. Flintstone!" said Rock. "In two weeks your kids will be the biggest thing in show-biz since the Termites!"

"Yabba-Dabba-Doo!" cried Fred.

Pebbles and Bamm-Bamm were an overnight success! Teens flocked to concerts to hear them! Reporters hounded the Flintstones' home. Every major magazine had a cover story featuring the world's newest singing sensations! Even Professor Freudstone ran experiments on the kids to see what made them sing!

An exhausted Fred returned home from work the next day. "Wilma! What's for dinner?" asked a hungry Fred.

"Who's got time to cook?" Wilma asked. "Take Barney and get a sandwich at the bowling alley! We're going to New Rock in the morning! The kids are going to appear on the Jay Lava Show!"

With the girls and kids gone, Fred and Barney had plenty of time to go golfing now. "We've got it made!" Fred said. "No wives or kids around the house making a racket!"

"So how come we're so miserable?" Barney asked.

Fred missed the ball again. "Let's face it, Barn. I miss Wilma and Pebbles!"

"And I miss Betty and Bamm-Bamm," sighed Barney.

After a week dragged by, Wilma, Betty and the kids finally returned home from their tour, with some exciting news for Fred and Barney. "Pebbles and Bamm-Bamm are going to make a movie! Isn't it wonderful?" Betty told the boys.

"We leave for Eurock tonight, right after the kids perform at the Hollyrock Palace!" said Wilma.

"Now just a doggone minute!" yelled Fred. "Pebbles is not going to Eurock! I absolutely forbid it!" But the girls were already gone!

"That does it, Barney!" Fred said. "It's time for K.O.O.K.! Kidnap Our Own Kids!"

Fred donned a trench coat, a hat and fake moustache. "You look awful silly in that disguise, Fred," said Barney. "This is how they do it on TV, Barn!" replied Fred. "Now remember — I snatch, you drive!"

Once inside the Hollyrock Palace, Fred grabbed Pebbles and Bamm-Bamm out of the arms of Rock Kidd. "Finster Brinkley's the name, Department of Education," Fred said in a low-pitched voice. "These kids aren't going anywhere except to school!"

"At two years old?" Rock asked.

"There's something familiar about that man," Betty said.

Wilma and Betty stared at the moustache and hat.

Before Fred could stop them, Pebbles pulled off the moustache, and Bamm-Bamm knocked off his hat.

"Fred!" Wilma screamed.

Fred took off running, a kid in each arm.

"Get going, pal! Let's get out of here!" Fred yelled.

They took off, Barney behind the wheel. Rock, Wilma and Betty were close behind!

"Maybe I can lose 'em!" Barney said.

"Step on it!" Fred yelled.

Twists and turns they went, Rock Kidd close on their tail!

Fred and Barney took an exit and headed straight into a police roadblock! "It's no use, Fred!" Barney cried.

"They're not taking Pebbles and Bamm-Bamm!" yelled Fred over and over again.

"Fred, what do you think you're doing?" Wilma asked gently.

"Fred! Fred, wake up!"

Fred opened his eyes and awoke from his dream.

"Wilma? Where am I? What happened?"

"You must have fallen asleep, Fred."

Wilma held up a little pink ballet dress. "Look, Fred! Isn't this cute? I bought it for Pebbles, for when she starts dancing lessons!"

"Absolutely not! No career for Pebbles! I'm not going through that again!" roared Fred Flintstone.

"What are you talking about?" asked Wilma.

"Oh, Wilma! I had the worst dream!" exclaimed Fred. "Pebbles became a famous star and I was miserable!"

Pebbles and Bamm-Bamm were once again playing with their toy instruments.

"Da-da-da-da!" said Pebbles.

"Bamm-Bamm! Bamm-Bamm-Bamm!" yelled Bamm-Bamm.

Fred and Wilma raced outside.

"You know, Wilma," said Fred as he was eyeing the instruments. "Being famous can be a ball, but it takes an adult to handle fame! Do you think I could be the next Elvis Prestone?"

And as Wilma, Pebbles and Bamm-Bamm covered their ears, Fred picked up Pebbles' toy guitar and started strumming, screeching the song from his dream: "*Open Up Your Heart And Let The Sun Shine In!!! Yabba-Dabba-Doo!!!*"

"Oh, brother!" sighed Wilma.

The end!

A Clue For Scooby-Doo!

Story by Dandi Mackall & Scott Awley

Illustrated by Scott Jeralds and Darryl Goudreau

"Here it is gang, Rocky Point Beach!" Fred announced.

"What a groovy place for a late night beach party!" Daphne said.

"Yeah, man, I can already taste those chocolate-covered hotdogs!" Shaggy crowed.

"Ree, roo!" Scooby-Doo agreed.

Since the beach was deserted, the kids had their pick of picnic spots. After cooking the first of the hotdogs, Shaggy noticed the gang was one member short. "Hey!" he said. "Like, where's Scooby-Doo? He's supposed to be helping me!"

Velma looked up from her book. "He went moon-surfing," she replied.

"Rooby-rooby-roo!" Scooby yelled from the ocean. Unfortunately, instead of catching a wave, his paw caught a glowing ghost in deep-sea diving gear!

"Groooooan!" moaned the spooky diver.

"Ripes!" Scooby yelped, quickly spinning the surfboard and dog-paddling back to shore!

The seaweed-covered ghost stepped out of the water. "Mooaaaaannnn!"

"Zoinks! A sea-going spook!" Shaggy yelled, hiding inside Velma's beach umbrella.

"You can relax, Shag... he's gone," Fred told him. "But he did leave behind one clue."

"Glowing footprints!" Daphne said. "I wonder what's behind this mystery!"

"Listen to this," Fred said the next day. "Another boat vanishes! Coast Guard baffled!"

"I wonder if the missing boats are connected to that spooky diver we saw?" Daphne asked.

Fred continued to read the newspaper. "Fisherman Ebenezer Shark claims this is the work of the ghost of Captain Cutler!"

"Let's pay this Shark a visit!" Velma said.

Ebenezer Shark was eager to talk, and invited the gang into his vessel. "Aye, I seen the ghost of Captain Cutler! A ghostly glow moving through the fog," Shark said in a raspy whisper, his sinister eyes narrowing down to tiny dots. "Months ago, Cutler's boat collided with one of those fancy yachts from the marina, sending him down to the graveyard of ships. As he vanished beneath the waves, Captain Cutler vowed he'd return and get his revenge."

A series of barks interrupted the story.

Down in the hold, Scooby had discovered a familiar-looking diving suit!

"Your pooch stumbled onto me old gear," Shark said, helping to free the dog. "If you want more about Cutler, see his wife up at the old lighthouse."

"There's something mighty fishy about Ebenezer Shark," Velma said after they left the boat.

"Yeah, he looks more like a barracuda!" Shaggy cracked.

"Daph and I will keep an eye on Shark," Fred said. "You three talk to the widow Cutler."

At the lighthouse entrance, Shaggy, Scooby and Velma were involved in a debate:

"Go ahead, Scoob—knock on the door," Shaggy said.

Scooby whimpered, holding his paw as if it were injured.

"Look at him!" Velma laughed. "What a ham!"

"Looks more like a chicken to me!" Shaggy retorted.

Inside the gloomy lighthouse, Shaggy, Velma and Scooby looked for Cutler's widow.

"Like, wow! This place is furnished like a Halloween store!" Shaggy said.

"Thank you, dearie!" a high-pitched voice cackled, making Shaggy jump into Scooby's arms. "We witches adore a haunted atmosphere!"

"We're here about Captain Cutler... we think we saw his ghost!" Velma explained.

"You did! I used my witchcraft to bring my husband back from a watery grave!"

"Whew!" Shaggy said, breathing a sigh of relief once he was outside the lighthouse. "Am I glad to get out of that scary pad! I don't want any spells cast on me!"

"If she's a witch, I'm a hobgoblin," Velma snorted. "Our next step to solving this mystery is to find Captain Cutler's ghost."

Shaggy pointed at the beach. "I think he's found us—check it out!" A glowing mass of yellow-green seaweed was inching along the edge of the beach! However, before they could grab it, the glow vanished into a drainpipe.

After eating a Scooby Snack for courage, Scooby dove into the pipe and pulled out the glowing clump of seaweed. An angry mouse was hanging onto the other end! The two struggled in a tug-of-war before the rodent gave up.

"Looks like you found a clue, Scooby-Doo!" Velma said.

Rejoining the others, Velma used her biology book to identify the seaweed. "This type is found only in the Graveyard of Ships," she read.

"That's where Captain Cutler went down!" Daphne said.

"Maybe that's where we'll find his ghost—and an answer to this mystery," Fred said. "Shark left about an hour ago. I think we need to go for an on-site inspection!"

After suiting up in rented scuba gear, the gang took their motorboat to the Graveyard of Ships.

"If we're going to find that ghost, we'd better split up," Fred said.

One by one they dove over the side, swimming to the bottom where numerous wrecked ships rested on the ocean floor like broken tombstones scattered across a cemetery.

Looking through a porthole, Daphne spotted a seated figure at a cabin table wearing an old style diving helmet. Swimming inside, Fred, Daphne and Velma soon found the suit to be a rusty relic from an earlier time, but before they could turn to leave, the door slammed behind them and was bolted shut!

"Oh, no! We're trapped," Velma said.

Meanwhile, Scooby had found another clue. Inside the hold of an old ship, Scooby was looking at shelves of air tanks. Some of the tanks were empty, but most had a full charge of air.

"This is somebody's private storeroom of scuba tanks!" Shaggy told him.

Unfortunately for the pair, the owner picked this moment to show up in all of his glowing glory!

"Zoinks! Captain Creepy! Swim for it, Scoob!"

Shaggy and Scooby weaved in and out of the many wrecked ships, searching for a place to hide.

"Over there!" Shaggy said, pointing to a closed cabin door.

Busting their way inside, they were surprised to discover Fred, Velma and Daphne!

"Nice save!" Fred exclaimed.

"Look at this," Daphne said. "More footprints!"

Following the trail, the gang soon discovered the glowing tracks came to a stop in front of a rock wall. "I'm pooped from all this swimming," Shaggy said, sitting on a rock that triggered a secret entrance into the cliff! Swimming through the passage, the gang found fresh air when they broke the surface of the water... along with what appeared to be a small fleet of stolen boats, many of them with fresh coats of paint to disguise their identities!

"We're in a giant underground cavern!" Shaggy exclaimed. "Get a load of all those yachts!"

"I guess this wraps up our mystery," Daphne noted, "if we can wrap up that ghost."

Fred grinned. "Not wrap him up—wash him up!"

Fred's plan to capture the ghost of Captain Cutler was simple. First, attract the spook's attention to a ramp located at one end of the cavern. When the ghost arrives, use a high-pressure fire hose from one of the yachts to blast him down the ramp and into a waiting net. Velma was in charge of the water control, while Fred and Daphne held the hose. Shaggy and Scooby waited at the net.

As planned, the ghost of Captain Cutler appeared at the top of the ramp. Velma turned on the water, but the slippery hose moved like a bucking bronco, spraying water in all directions. Scooby took the brunt of the blast, which knocked him into a small motorboat that sped around the cavern out of control. Shooting up the ramp, dog and boat flew into the air like a rocket!

"Rooby-rooby-roo!" Scooby yelled as the craft plummeted downward, smashing over the top of the ghost and pinning the spook's arms to his sides.

"Well, let's see if we've caught ourselves a Shark," Fred said, removing the ghost's diving helmet. However, the face revealed underneath belonged to a man none of them recognized!

Then, Shaggy picked up a piece of seaweed. Holding it to the man's chin, he asked, "Does this help remind you of a certain picture we saw on the widow Cutler's wall?"

"Captain Cutler!" Velma said.

"My perfect scheme—ruined, thanks to you meddling kids!" Cutler sneered.

The next day, the gang gathered for grape sodas.

"That was some plan Captain Cutler and his wife had!" Fred said. "Spreading the phony story about Cutler's boat sinking and then stealing the boats from the marina was one deep-sea hoax."

"Too bad for him his diving suit got covered in that kooky glowing seaweed," Shaggy agreed.

"I guess that wraps up another mystery," Velma said, before being interrupted by a loud slurp!

"Gee whiz, Scoob—I think you need a refill," Shaggy said.

Scooby disagreed. As the dog gave a final giant sip on his straw, the other four glasses on the table emptied like magic!

"How did Scooby do that?" Daphne wondered.

"I guess that's another mystery," Fred replied.

Scooby smacked his lips and grinned. A mystery, yes—and he wasn't telling!

The end!

TOM and JERRY ™

ROLLER COASTER RODENT

Story by Sara Hoagland Hunter
Adaptation by Scott Redman
Illustrated by Renegade Animation & Colorgrafix

Jerry is out for a run with Tom, which means that Tom is chasing Jerry again. Jerry makes a dash for the amusement park. He would really like to take Tom for a ride. And an amusement park is so much better for two than for one.

Jerry hops onto the log-on-water ride. Tom follows. But before he can get at Jerry, the helpful lumber-jack straps him in. *Really* straps him in. Jerry gets ready for some fun. Tom isn't going anywhere—even if he wants to.

You're going to like this, Tom. It's the biggest log-jam ride in the world with the most awesome vertical drop on the planet. The logs actually approach the speed of sound! Don't worry, Tom. Everything's going to be just fine. Oh, and you might get a little wet when this thing hits the water at 100 miles per hour.

Go ahead, Tom, follow Jerry. He wants you to relax after that rough ride. Just lean up against this board here and don't worry about a thing. That flashing light? Someone is just taking a picture. Of what? Jerry will show you later, and everyone else you know, too. Rested? Good, because Jerry knows the perfect thing to do next.

Bumper cars are just the thing to get rid of the blues. Hey, you bully, stop bumping so hard! That's right, knock it off—Tom's not scared of you. He will teach you a lesson. You think you're tough? Well, keep it up and Tom will really let you have it! Right, Tom?

Okay, Tom, I think he's had enough. That was nice of you to take it easy on him. Believe me, he won't be back again soon. He's exhausted from beating you up. Gosh, there are a lot of stars out today. All of them seem to be circling your head, Tom.

Tom *does* want to teach Jerry a lesson—up close and personal!
Jerry signals Tom to come on up and catch him, if he can. Go ahead,
Tom. Teach him a lesson. Follow him right over the wall to...

THE CHILDREN'S PETTING ZOO! A mob of kids want to pet Tom. "Here kitty, kitty!" "Good kitty, look at the pretty kitty!" "I wanna hug the kitty!" "I wanna chase him!" "I wanna squeeze him till he turns blue!" "I want to throw him up to the sky and see if he lands on his feet!"

Wow, that is the sweetest smelling stuff in the whole wide world. There's no way any self-respecting cat can resist cotton candy. Tom sniffs the sweet candy smell. He leans further and further over the bowl to get a real nose full.

Jerry comes up from behind. Tippy-toe, tippy-toe, he must be quiet. He doesn't want to spoil Tom's surprise. He wants to help Tom get more cotton candy than he ever hoped for. Ready, Tom? Bottoms up!

Jerry waits patiently as Tom takes several hundred turns around the candy-spinning bowl. Finally it stops and he comes out. Tom's got so much cotton candy he's even wearing it as a hat. Jerry wants a bite of Tom's hat. Tom wants to give him a bite, but not of the hat.

Jerry races down the row of food stands. He runs past the hotdogs and the ice cream. Tom's almost got his hands on him, but the mouse jumps up on a tank. Tom leaps, Jerry steps away, and SPLOOOSH! Tom lands right in the tank—full of lemonade. Jerry thinks Tom is lucky; fresh lemonade is DEEEELISH!.

Tom drags himself out of the tank and looks high and low but Jerry's disappeared. Where is that mouse? He'll pay for that lemonade bath! Then Tom is distracted by an attendant who announces, "Free rides on the most exciting roller coaster in the world! All aboard! Free rides!" Tom's favorite word is "free."

Uh-oh! The attendant is really Jerry! Looks like this ride is going to be free for everyone except Tom. What price will he have to pay?

This is a problem—the coaster needed a few repairs. Look at that cat fly! "Just when we thought we were safe up here, now the cats are flying, too," thinks the bird. He is very relieved when he sees Tom keep going.

Wham! Bam! The kids love the cat-smashing effect on the ferris wheel. They think it's part of the ride. Tom thinks that the ferris wheel is now part of his face.

Down, down, down, down goes Tom, falling like a lead balloon. The park sure looks little from up here. But it sure is getting bigger the faster he falls. SQUAOOSH! He lands on something nice and soft. He made it! He's safe and sound! He opens his eyes and sees that he has landed safely—on the back of the BUMPER-BOAT BULLY!!

As Jerry watches them float into the tunnel, something tells him that it won't be the Tunnel of Love this trip. But on the other hand, the park is so much more fun for two than for one.

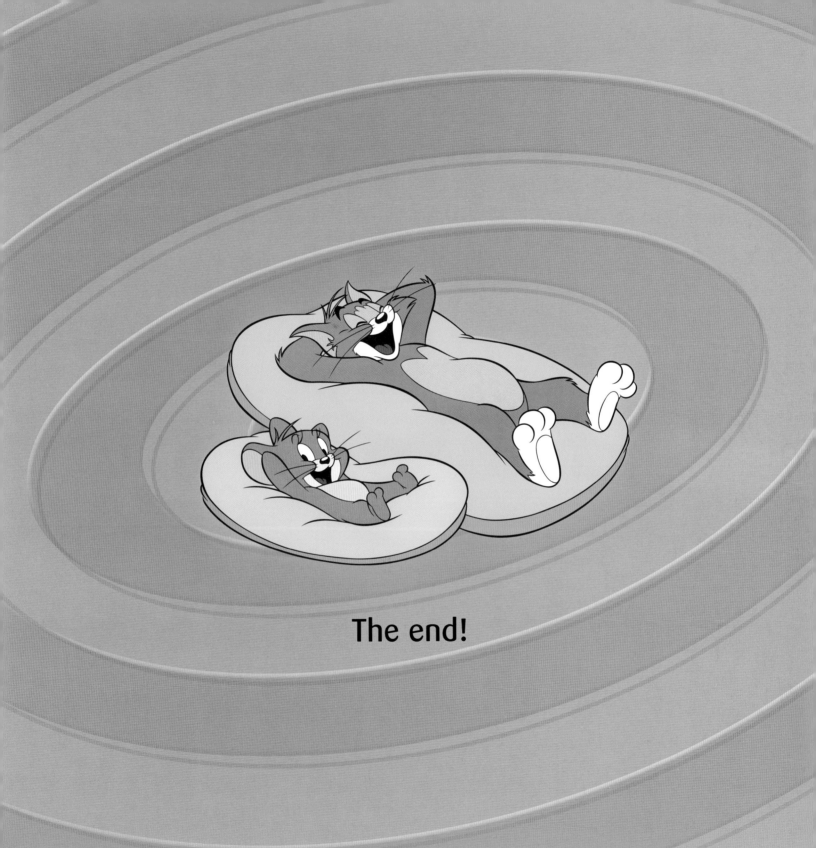

The end!

Jet Settin' Astro

Story adapted by Peggy Shaw

Pencils by Iwao Takamoto

Color illustrations by Darryl Goudreau

Astro was the happiest dog in the universe. He had everything he wanted... a great family, he lived in a cozy pad, and he enjoyed nice long walks with George.

Just then, the doorbell rang. When George opened the door, a stout little man swaggered in.

"Mr. Jetson?" he said. "My name is Withers and I represent a very rich client, Mr. J.P. Gottrockets. I am looking for his lost dog... and it looks as though I have found him!"

"Astro?" gulped George.

"Is that dog 5-feet, 9-inches tall? Does he weigh 115 pounds and answer to the name 'Tralfaz'?" Withers asked.

"Tralfaz?" George and Astro said together.

"Rukk!" added Astro.

"Yes, indeed, *Tralfaz*," Withers said. "He is Mr. Gottrockets' dog, and I am here to take him home. Tralfaz lives in the fanciest glass doghouse in the galaxy, with a solar-heated pool and his own fire hydrants—and all the Moondoggie treats he can eat! It's a life of canine luxury!"

"You don't want that life-of-luxury jazz, do you, Astro?" Judy asked sadly.

But Astro just cocked his head, starry-eyed. "Ruh-HUH!" he barked.

And off he went with Withers.

At the Gottrockets mansion, Tralfaz truly was the luckiest mutt in the universe. He had everything a dog could want—a push-button chair, big, ham bones, and fruity drinks with lots of fizz. But was he happy?

Not really.

Not until one day when he was paid a visit...

"Reorge!" Astro barked.

"Hey, pal!" said Geroge, as Astro gave him a big slurp.

"I Ruv Roo!"

"We love you, too," said Jane, Elroy and Judy.

Astro showed off his satellite phone and new clothes from the canine designer "Fideaux."

"That's quite a hat," George laughed. "I wonder what my boss would say if I wore this to work at the Spacely Space Sprockets Factory!"

Just then, Mr. Gottrockets drove up in his red, jet-powered bubble car and saw everyone having fun.

"Just look at them, Withers," he said, with a sigh. "It was wrong to take Tralfaz from the Jetsons. Give him a nice, big steak and tell them they can take Tralfaz—I mean Astro—home."

"Right away, sir," Withers said.

"Mr. Jetson, Mr. Gottrockets is giving you the dog as a gift," Withers announced, as Astro pounced on the little man, knocking him to the ground.

"Down, boy!" Withers pleaded. "Yeowtch! That's the fifth pair of pants you've ruined this week!"

"Come on, boy," George said to Astro. "Let's go home!"

"Rip-pee!" barked Astro.

"Rip-pee—I mean, Yippee!" Withers agreed.

And all the way home the Jetsons sang, *"For he's a jolly good fellow, for he's a jolly good fellow..."*

And Astro barked, *"Ror Re's a Rolly Rood Rell-ow..."*

"Which nobody can deny!"

The end!

YOGI BEAR™

HOME SWEET JELLYSTONE

Story adapted by Peggy Shaw

Pencils by Iwao Takamoto

Color illustrations by Darryl Goudreau

It was a sunny day at Jellystone National Park when a car suddenly chugged through the gate with a message for Ranger John Smith. He opened it in his office and read it out loud to his assistant.

Chief Ranger Smith, your Uncle Charlie has left you his fortune, but to claim it you must live in his mansion.

"Do you have any idea what this means?" said the Ranger excitedly. "No more babbling brooks! No more finding lost kids or putting out forest fires! And above all, NO MORE YOGI BEAR!"

"You called, Sir?" Yogi said, leaning through the cabin window.

"Yogi! Read this message!"

Yogi stared at it in disbelief. "But, Mr. Ranger! This means you're leaving the park!"

"I'm leaving *you*, Yogi," Ranger Smith said. "You've caused me nothing but trouble!"

"Well, Sir, we bears were here first and got along better without you Rangers!" Yogi exclaimed.

"I'm glad to know how you feel," the Ranger said angrily. "Good riddance! And if I never see another bear again, it'll be too soon!"

Later that day, Yogi and Boo Boo watched as Ranger Smith packed and left Jellystone Park.

"I'm going to miss Mr. Ranger, Yogi," said Boo Boo sadly.

"Me too, Little Buddy—like ya miss a toothache!" Yogi replied.

"Hee-yuh-hay! Come on. Let's raid some pic-a-nic tables!"

But life was no picnic for Ranger Smith at his Uncle Charlie's mansion.

No redwood trees, no campfires, and no cookouts. The Ranger missed playing baseball with his friends, skipping stones in the river and showing off Jellystone's world-famous geyser, Old Fitful.

He even missed— BEARS!

Jellystone's number-one Ranger sat in the big house all alone, thinking about life without Yogi.

"I should be happy!" he muttered. "But I can't stop thinking about Jellystone! Still... two weeks without a single letter. Well, if they don't miss me, I won't miss them!"

Back at Jellystone, life had changed for Yogi and Boo Boo, too.
Yogi hadn't eaten in days—no peanut butter and jelly sandwiches, deviled eggs or chocolate cake. Not even a drop of honey.
And Boo Boo was worried.

Over at the station, the assistant was on the phone to Mr. Ranger...

"Boo Boo's fine, Chief," the assistant was saying. "But I'm worried about Yogi. He won't eat!"

"My plan has worked!" Yogi said with a grin. "Hey, hey, hey! Let's be on our way!"

"Where to?" asked Boo Boo, confused.

"To meet Mr. Ranger!"

"But how do you know he'll come?"

"Because Mr. Ranger is one of the good guys, Boo Boo."

And sure enough, Ranger Smith raced out of his mansion and headed straight for Jellystone National Park.

All the way he fretted to himself, "Poor Yogi, dragging himself around the forest! Of course, I'd come to the rescue of any dumb animal."

And as the Ranger drove through Jellystone's gate, Yogi threw himself in the road, moaning.

"You poor bear!" the Ranger cried, rushing to Yogi's side. "I should never have left you, Yogi, but I'm back! I'll have you up and around in no time! Lots of rest and good food will do it!" the Ranger said, heaving the big bear over one shoulder.

"How about pic-a-nic baskets, Sir?" Yogi suggested weakly.

"Sure, Yogi," the Ranger agreed. "Lots of pincic baskets until you get your strength back."

"There's one thing you gotta admit about Yogi," Boo Boo said, as they walked away. "For a dumb animal, he's sure smarter than the average Ranger!"

The end!

TOM and JERRY™

LIGHTS, CAMERA, YEEOOOOWCH!

Story adapted by Charles Carney
Illustrated by Tim Cahill and Ryan Dunlavey

HOLLYWOOD! The place where movies and magic are made!

The place where gorillas climb skyscrapers, where the seas part, where volcanoes erupt—but only when a director *says* so. Where anything but anything can happen. A place, in fact, where...

...even a cat can—if he works really hard—become a star. *Even* if he has to start at the bottom, chasing mice.

But while Tom was watching a cowboy movie on the television, Jerry interrupted him by unplugging it.

Jerry made sure Tom would have trouble chasing him, but his effort wasn't quite enough.

Through the door, over the fence, and into a taxi, Tom chased the quick little mouse. Then into the city to the Bighouse Cinema.

Tom stood looking around for Jerry when he heard a whistle and saw the mouse run behind a movie screen playing a big Hollywood musical. Tom watched the screen. *I could do that*, he thought. Then he ran after Jerry again.

It was dark behind the screen. Tom squinted, then heard another whistle. Whenever Jerry whistled like that, it made Tom even angrier! He looked up to see Jerry in the curtain ropes w—a—a—a—y above the floor. It's a well-known fact that cats are good climbers.

Most cats, anyway.

Of course, Jerry always wanted to be a director, and he saw the perfect actor in Tom. If only Tom would chase him, he could direct him in all kinds of movie roles!

Tom wasn't about to let this little troublemaker move him around. He took a mighty leap at the little pest, but he leaped a little too hard...

...hitting the screen with a WHAP! Wait! It wasn't the screen—or was it? It looked an awful lot like a door. Tom stepped through it.

It was a dark room. A neon sign flashed outside. Tom saw the word DETECTIVE painted on the glass pane on the door.

A detective? In a movie theater? Then he heard a gunshot! A woman screamed! Police sirens wailed! What would Tom do?

He heard a familiar whistle. "Grrrr...!"

Tom stepped to the window and realized he was on the 20th floor! Jerry stood at the window of the building across the way, sticking out his tongue. He pointed to a washing line between the buildings as if he were inviting Tom across. Tom untied his end of the line. He clutched the cord, stepped back into the room, then ran toward the open window, closed his eyes...

...and jumped! *"YEEEEEAAAAAAHOOOOOOOOOY!!!!"*

Yes! Tom was truly in the movies now, although he didn't know how it was happening. A detective film! He looked down, but instead of the street, he was swinging over a jungle river!

The cord had become a vine in his hands. Crocodiles snapped at his feet! Then an ape-man swung past him. "Move over!" shouted the man. "The jungle's no place for cats!"

How is this happening? Tom thought, as he swung out and into...
...a Spanish courtyard tower! Tom went through the window and
crashed onto a table. The top flew off and out another window.

He *f—l—e—w* through the air. **SPLAAAAASH!**
Everything became still as he bobbed on the table top in the
water. Then a huge fin sliced through the water right next to him.

SNAP! SNARL! SNAP! SNAP! Shark!

Jerry floated by on a tiny sailboat. He waved to Tom, who began to paddle like a surfer after the mouse, mad that Jerry was getting away but even more concerned with keeping ahead of the hungry shark. Jerry disappeared. Tom looked over his shoulder for the shark, but what did he see instead but...

...the dark blue ocean rising up behind him! "TIDAL WAVE!" someone screamed! Tom stood on the table top and rode the wave as best he could, which wasn't very good at all, since cats aren't fond of water.

Seaweed tangled in his ears, flowing in the wind like long, green hair. The wave rose higher and higher! Tom held his balance for dear life! *I'd give anything to be on solid ground right now*, he thought. *Anything!*

WHAM! Tom brushed the seaweed from his eyes to see that he was sitting in the back seat of a strange, huge black vehicle.

A man in a hooded cape sat in the front seat. "Hold it," the man's masked assistant yelled. "There's some joker in the back seat!"

"Joker?" said the driver gravely. "Let's go!" The car's wheels squealed and they took off, from a standstill to 100 miles per hour! As they went down the road, Tom saw Jerry waving good-bye at the curb.

Tom grabbed the cape billowing in the breeze and hung on... like a leaf in the wind, and he sailed through the air and landed... on some theater seats!

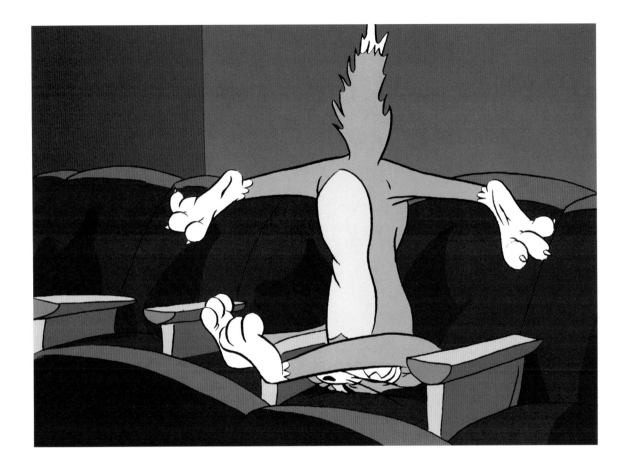

When he looked up to the screen, the car was speeding off into the distance. The audience cheered. Tom was so happy to be in a familiar place that he cheered, too. Then he felt a tap on his shoulder. An usher grabbed him by the collar.

"You don't have a ticket!" the usher growled. And he hauled Tom to the door and threw him into the street.

Under the seat, Jerry settled down with a box of popcorn and enjoyed the rest of the show. *Too bad* this theater has only ten screens, he chuckled to himself. *Tom might have been a great action star!* Jerry was happy that he'd helped his friend Tom get into the movies. And we do mean *into the movies!*

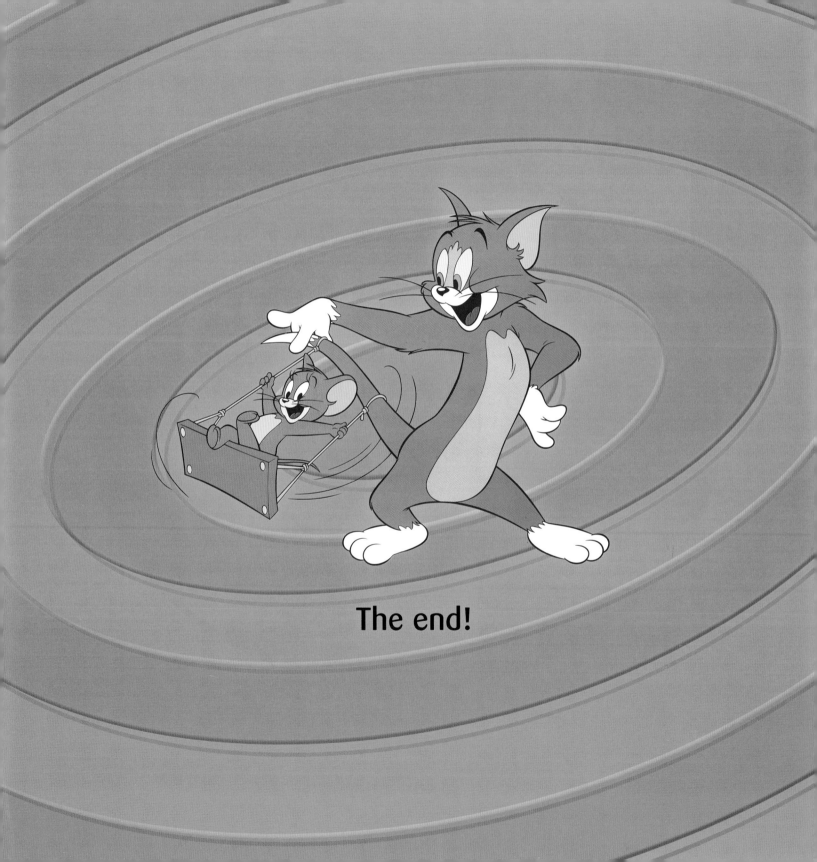

The end!